BUNDER THE BACKYARD SKY

Published by
PEACHTREE PUBLISHERS, LTD.
494 Armour Circle NE
Atlanta, Georgia 30324

Design and typography by Laurie Shock
Photographic backgrounds on pages 6 and 7, and pages 24 and 25 were provided by Peter Beney. The animal closeups on pages 8 and 9, and 14 and 15 were provided by Joe Sebo. These are photographs of animals at Zoo Atlanta, where Mr. Sebo is staff photographer. The remaining photographic backgrounds were provided by Stan Mullins.

Manufactured in China

10 9 8 7 6 5 4 3 2 1

Library of Congress Cataloging-in-Publication Data

Shulman, Neil.
    Under the backyard sky / Neil Shulman and Sibley Fleming
Illustrations by Stan Mullins.
        p.   cm.
    Summary: Lonely Lucy is jealous of the time her father, a heart surgeon, spends away from home, but when he brings a Maasai girl to America for surgery, both girls find a cure for their particular type of heartsickness.
        ISBN 1-56145-093-6 : $13.95
        [1. Loneliness—Fiction. 2. Father and daughters—Fiction.
3. Physicians—Fiction. 4. Maasai (African people)—Fiction.]
I. Fleming, Sibley. II. Mullins, Stan, ill. III. Title.
PZ7 .S55947Un   1995
[Fic]—dc20   95-19761
                                                                    CIP
                                                                    AC

B UNDER THE BACKYARD SKY

Neil Shulman and Sibley Fleming

Illustrations by
Stan Mullins

PEACHTREE
ATLANTA

Picture books are good for lots of things. Like when your dad goes on a long trip and doesn't take you, you can look at the pictures and imagine where your dad is. You see, my dad is the only family I have, and he's always working. So I spend a lot of time looking at my picture books.

Anyhow, that's how I got to know so much about Kenya, a country in Africa. My dad is a heart surgeon and he goes there sometimes. He works with doctors who fly into remote places where there are no hospitals.

A heart surgeon fixes broken hearts. The best way to explain what that means is to tell you what my dad tells me. "A heart is like a house with four rooms and four doors. When the doors don't open or close all the way, or there is a hole in the walls between rooms, a heart is broken."

6

When my dad went to Kenya, I stared
real hard at the pictures in my picture
book. I stared so hard that soon I could
see the herds of animals running off the
pages. I imagined a plane at the top of
the page with my dad inside it.

I read about all the tribes in Kenya and how each one has its own language. The tribes can talk to each other since they have one language that they all speak called Swahili. I think I would like to learn some words in Swahili too.

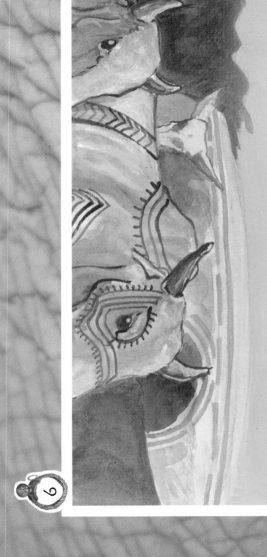

I was especially interested in reading about a tribe called the Maasai because my dad told me he would visit them. From my books I learned that they raise cattle and that they are proud warriors.

Dad said the Maasai were different. They like their own way of doing things. They have no interest in modern life in the big cities of Africa. I thought a lot about the Maasai after my father left.

Dad was in Kenya for two weeks. It seemed like forever. When he finally got home, he was in a big hurry to leave again, almost as soon as he walked in the door. He didn't even have time to unpack.

"Sorry, Lucy, I have to rush to the hospital to get ready for a young visitor," he said. But he didn't have time to explain.

"Here's a surprise for you, Lucy," my dad said, handing me a doll from his bag.

"Who made this silly old doll?" I asked as if there was a sour grape on my tongue. "I don't need home-made dolls. I have lots of fancy dolls already."

I was mad. I thought he gave the doll to me because he was too busy to put it away.

"Mind the sitter while I'm gone." That's all he could say as he rushed around. He didn't even hear what I said.

11

Then we heard a knock on our door. When my dad opened it, there were warriors with spears on our front porch! And they were dressed just like the people in my picture book!

"This is a Maasai doctor. He is called a Laibon in their language," I could hear my dad saying. And then the Laibon shook a rattling stick at me. I was sort of scared.

"Why are these people here?" I asked.

12

I listened quietly as my dad told me the story: He said, "I met the Laibon near the Maasai village. He was bandaging a wounded warrior and I went over to see if I could help him. When we were finished, he told me about a little girl in his village whose heart was very sick. I went with him to visit the girl.

Her name was Annah."

Then my dad told about meeting Annah: "She was outside a big tent sitting very very quietly. I listened to her heart with my stethoscope. I could tell one of the doors of her heart was stuck shut." Daddy told Annah's mother that Annah needed a heart operation which couldn't be done there. But if they brought her to the United States he could operate.

Annah's mother was worried about her going far away from her home in Maasailand. My dad suggested that she bring her family so she wouldn't be afraid.

"I didn't know she was related to everyone in the village," he laughed.

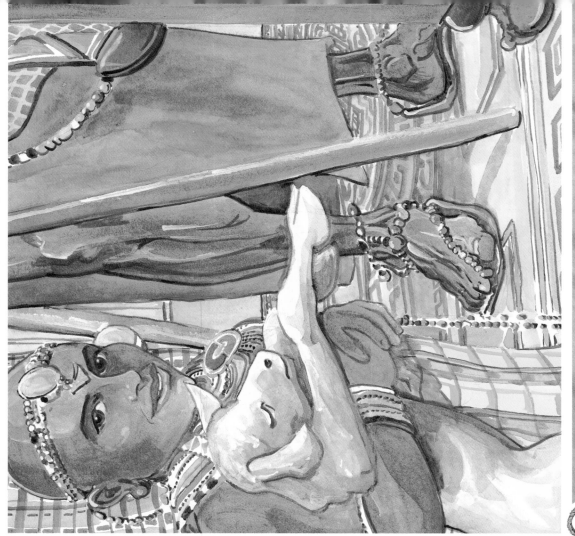

The Laibon spoke up after my father finished his story. He had a very deep voice like the pit of a volcano. "The whole village cares about Annah. We didn't want her to be lonely, so we all came."

A little girl holding a goat stepped out from behind the Laibon and smiled. "So this is Annah," I thought. "She doesn't look very sick to me."

19

The Maasai did not want to stay in our house. They said they liked the trees and earth around them and the sky up over their heads.

Well, in the next few days, they set up a whole village in our backyard. It was fun for a while, but I began to miss my father again. He was busy looking after Annah at the hospital.

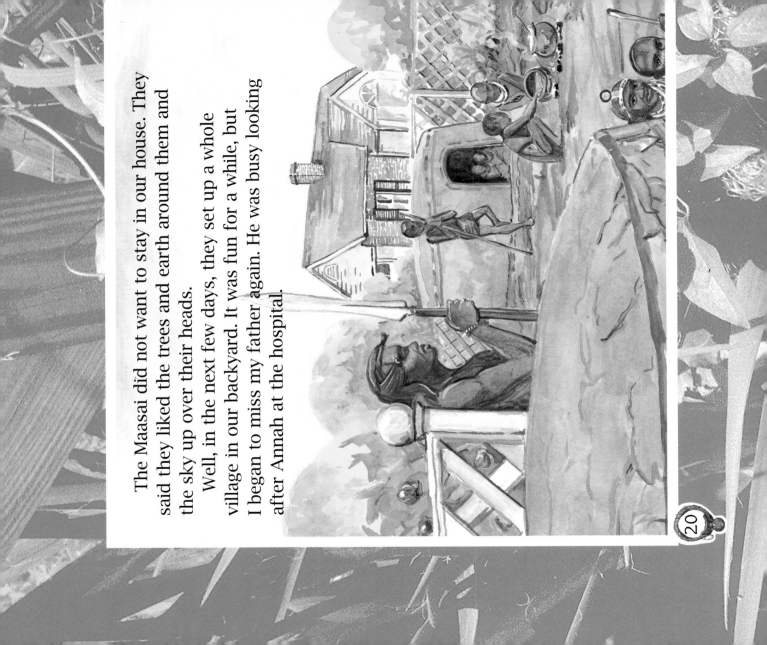

And I was getting pretty tired of being alone all the time. I went into our backyard to look for someone to play with. I banged on a hut, but nothing happened. Then I kicked dirt on a picture a little kid was making. I was just getting ready to tip over a bowl of wash water when I saw the Laibon.

"Lucy," the Laibon said, "Why is your heart so angry?"

I tried not to cry. But I was so sad that I just started to tell him how my daddy was too busy for me.

"Now that he's home, he's spending all of his time with you and Annah. And I hate it," I said. "Annah has a whole village as her family! It's not fair." I was really crying now, and I thought I wouldn't be able to stop.

The Laibon bent down and looked into my eyes. "I'm sure what you say is true, Lucy. Your father is spending time with Annah because she needs an operation. Perhaps your father shows his love for you through the good things he does for others."

"I'm...not...sure," I said, choking on my words.

"I don't think I am the person you should be talking to," said the Laibon.

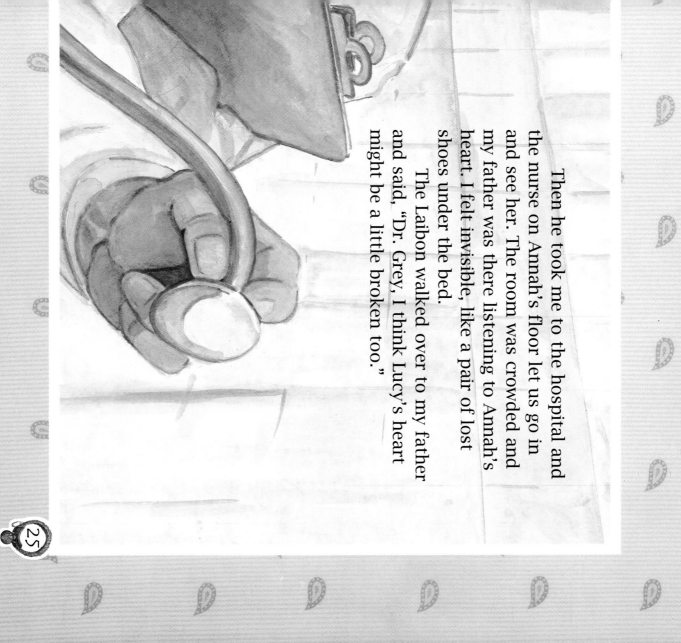

Then he took me to the hospital and the nurse on Annah's floor let us go in and see her. The room was crowded and my father was there listening to Annah's heart. I felt invisible, like a pair of lost shoes under the bed.

The Laibon walked over to my father and said, "Dr. Grey, I think Lucy's heart might be a little broken too."

All of a sudden, I knew what I wanted to say. I tugged on my father's coat. "Bend down so I can tell you something." My father knelt down next to me, looking a little worried. "I've really missed you, Dad," I said.

He didn't look worried at all then. In fact, he smiled a huge smile just at me and said, "I've really missed you too, Lucy." Then he hugged me tight, and just like magic, I wasn't sad anymore.

The Laibon stretched out his arms like he wanted to hug the whole room and smiled.

A few weeks later, Annah got to come home to her family in the backyard. I'm proud of my father for fixing Annah's heart, and I'm happy that my heart is feeling pretty good, too. We had a big Maasai party to celebrate, with a bonfire and drums. Annah and I got to play together and she even let me wear her necklace.

My dad said he and I would go on a trip, just the two of us! I was thinking about suggesting that we go to Maasailand, since the Laibon and Annah and her village were starting to seem like my family and I knew I would miss them when they left.

The Laibon told me that no matter how far away they were, to remember that the sky stretched all the way from our backyard to Africa. "We can always be together," he said, "under the backyard sky."

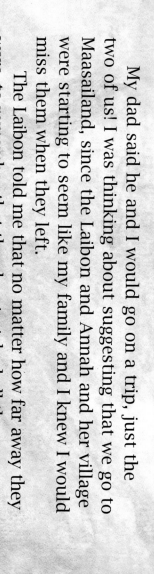

Unlike most ancient cultures, which have been tempted to replace their old customs with western technology and values, the Maasai want to keep their way of life.

When we grow up a certain way, our customs, or ways of living, do not seem unusual to us. This is what we mean by the word "culture." It includes the way we dress, what we eat, our religion, our language, our art, and many other things about us.

Our culture is also affected by our environment. In the Maasai's environment, all kinds of wild animals live in the countryside. An elephant or giraffe, a lion or hyena, would not be a strange sight to the Maasai. North Americans only see these animals when we visit the zoo, so they are exotic to us. We have skyscrapers, fast food restaurants, and baseball teams. These would be exotic to the Maasai.

Maybe the most interesting thing about culture is that it teaches us to behave in different ways even though we are all the same in many respects.

If you could make up any kind of culture you wanted, what would it be like?

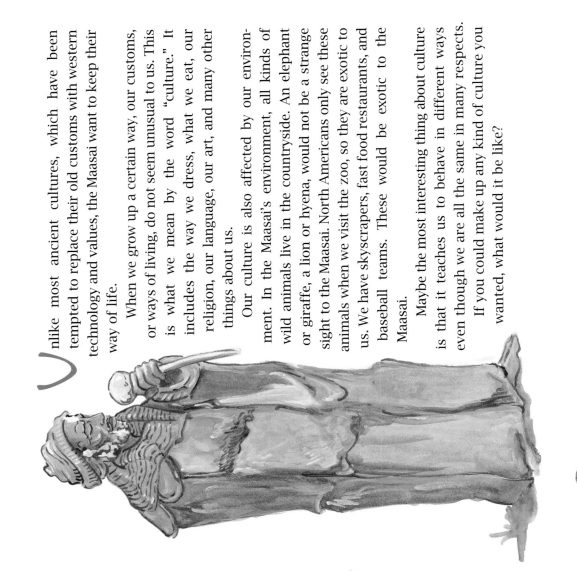

While Annah in this story is an imaginary character, there is a real organization called HEART TO HEART that brings sick children like Annah to the United States for surgery. HEART TO HEART started when Dr. Herman A. Taylor met a little girl named Faith on a trip to Kenya. Faith needed an operation on her heart to make her well, but the Kenyan hospitals did not have the equipment or the doctors to do the surgery. Dr. Taylor went home to America and raised the money to bring Faith, her mother, and her doctor to the United States for the operation. Then he decided to find other children like Faith who needed heart surgery, but couldn't get it. He called his new idea HEART TO HEART.

HEART TO HEART brings the sick child, a family member, and the child's doctor to the United States for the operation. The family member comes to keep the the child company, and the doctor comes to learn about new ideas to make other sick children well. Most of the visitors stay with an American family, who can learn from their guests about a different culture. So far, children have come from countries all over the world, including Kenya, Honduras, Nicaragua, Belarus, and Jamaica. If you would like more information about the HEART TO HEART program, please write to:

Heart to Heart

318 Lyons-Harrison Research Building
701 South 19th Street
Birmingham, AL 35294-0007